🕮 READERS

Level 1

Level 2

A Note to Parents

DK READERS is a compelling program for beginning readers, designed in conjunction with leading literacy experts, including Dr. Linda Gambrell, Distinguished Professor of Education at Clemson University. Dr. Gambrell has served as President of the National Reading Conference, the College Reading Association, and the International Reading Association.

Beautiful illustrations and superb full-color photographs combine with engaging, easy-to-read stories to offer a fresh approach to each subject in the series. Each DK READER is guaranteed to capture a child's interest while developing his or her reading skills, general knowledge, and love of reading.

The five levels of DK READERS are aimed at different reading abilities, enabling you to choose the books that are exactly right for your child:

Pre-level 1: Learning to read
Level 1: Beginning to read
Level 2: Beginning to read alone
Level 3: Reading alone
Level 4: Proficient readers

The "normal" age at which a child begins to read can be anywhere from three to eight years old. Adult participation through the lower levels is very helpful for providing encouragement, discussing storylines, and sounding out unfamiliar words.

No matter which level you select, you can be sure that you are helping your child learn to read, then read to learn!

LONDON, NEW YORK, MUNICH,
MELBOURNE, and DELHI

Senior Editor Victoria Taylor
Designer Sandra Perry
Senior Designer Anna Formanek
Design Manager Nathan Martin
Managing Editor Laura Gilbert
Publishing Manager Julie Ferris
Publishing Director Simon Beecroft
Pre-production Producer Rebecca Fallowfield
Producer Melanie Mikellides
Jacket Designer Jon Hall

Reading Consultant
Dr. Linda Gambrell PhD.

First American Edition, 2013
13 14 15 16 17 10 9 8 7 6 5 4 3 2 1

Published in the United States by DK Publishing
375 Hudson Street, New York, New York 10014

Page design copyright © 2013 Dorling Kindersley Limited

DK books are available at special discounts when purchased in bulk
for sales promotions, premiums, fund-raising, or educational use.
For details, contact: DK Publishing Special Markets,
375 Hudson Street, New York, New York 10014
SpecialSales@dk.com

A catalog record for this book is available
from the Library of Congress.

ISBN 978-1-4654-0174-8 (Paperback)
ISBN 978-1-4654-0175-5 (Hardback)

Color reproduction by Media Development and Printing, UK
Printed and bound in China by L.Rex

Discover more at
www.dk.com
www.LEGO.com

Contents

DK READERS

BEGINNING 1 TO READ

DC UNIVERSE™
SUPER HEROES

Ready for Action!

Written by Victoria Taylor

Super Heroes

The world is protected by a special group of super heroes.

Batman

Robin

Come and meet some of the
super heroes and see them
in action. . .

Superman

Wonder
Woman

Superman

This is Superman!

He can fly and has super-strength which gives him great power.

He keeps the city of Metropolis safe from villains.

cape

Wonder Woman

This is Wonder Woman!

She is very strong and very fast.

She has a secret weapon. It is a Lasso of Truth that makes criminals confess.

lasso

Robot Battle

Superman and Wonder Woman team up to defeat the villain Lex Luthor.

Lex Luthor is Superman's main enemy. The villain has a robot that he can sit inside and control.

Together Superman and Wonder Woman defeat the robot.

Bruce Wayne

This is Bruce Wayne!

Most people think that
Bruce is just rich and famous.

But Bruce leads an exciting
double-life as the super
hero Batman!

Bruce's
butler Alfred

suit

Come and meet Batman. . .

Batman

Batman protects the people of Gotham City from dangerous super-villains.

He wears a bullet-proof Batsuit that keeps him safe.

Batsuit

Robin

Batman does not battle Gotham City's crime alone. He has a partner called Robin.

Batman and Robin always look out for each other.

The Batcave

Welcome to the Batcave!
This is a secret cave hidden
under Batman's home.

He stores his vehicles here.
There is lots of equipment to
help Batman fight crime.

The Batmobile

This is the Batmobile.

It is Batman's favorite vehicle.

The Batmobile is very fast.

missile

It can fire missiles at Batman's enemies. Let's see it in action…

The Two-Face Chase

Batman is in his Batmobile.

He sees villain Two-Face driving away from the bank with a safe!

safe

Batman catches the crook and returns the safe to the bank where it belongs!

missile

The Batwing

This is the Batwing.
It is Batman's super-fast
airplane.

light

He uses it to defend Gotham City from the air.

Let's see it in action. . .

Batwing over Gotham

The Joker is attacking
Gotham City from the sky.

Batman arrives
in his
Batwing.

The Joker says he will let
off toxic laughing gas.

Batman fires missiles at
the Joker's helicopter
to stop him.

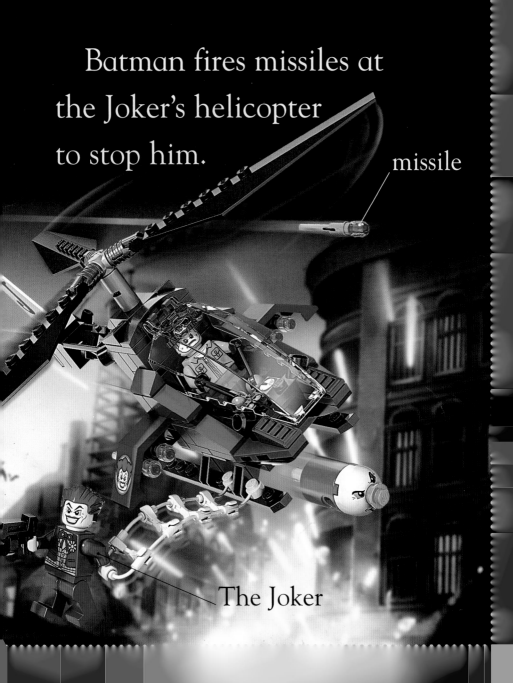

missile

The Joker

Catcycle Chase

Catwoman has stolen
a diamond.
She is escaping on
her motorbike.

Batman flies in
and throws his
Batarang. It knocks
the jewel out of
Catwoman's hand.

Catwoman is
no match
for Batman!

Batarang

Funhouse Escape

Three villains have caught Robin and trapped him in the Funhouse fairground ride. Can you see Robin?

Batman arrives in his Batcycle!

He rescues Robin and restores law and order to Gotham City.

A super hero has saved the
day again!

Glossary

Batarang
A weapon in the shape of a bat.

Batsuit
The special armored suit that Batman wears.

lasso
A rope with a loop at the end.

missile
An object that is shot at something.

safe
A strong metal box for storing valuable things.

Index

DK READERS

My name is

_____

I have read this book ☑

Date

_____